The Warrior's Song

Adam Howard

For the warriors who dare to sing in the valley.

TRULY SALTY
PUBLISHING

Dedication

For my Mema, Marion Williams,
who first taught me that worship is more than a melody —
it's a way of life.

For my mom, Sheila,
whose unwavering faith and love for music built an altar in our
home that still echoes in my heart today.

And for every warrior who lifts a song when the battle rages —
your worship changes everything.

Contents

The Original Battle Song

2 Chronicles 20:1–30

After this the Moabites and Ammonites, and with them some of the Meunites, came against Jehoshaphat for battle.

Some men came and told Jehoshaphat, "A great multitude is coming against you from Edom, from beyond the sea; and, behold, they are in Hazazon-tamar" (that is, Engedi).

Then Jehoshaphat was afraid and set his face to seek the Lord, and proclaimed a fast throughout all Judah.

And Judah assembled to seek help from the Lord; from all the cities of Judah they came to seek the Lord.

And Jehoshaphat stood in the assembly of Judah and Jerusalem, in the house of the Lord, before the new court, and said, "O Lord, God of our fathers, are you not God in heaven? You rule over all the kingdoms of the nations. In your hand are power and might, so that none is able to withstand you.

Did you not, our God, drive out the inhabitants of this land before your people Israel, and give it forever to the descendants of Abraham your friend?

And they have lived in it and have built for you in it a sanctuary for your name, saying,

'If disaster comes upon us, the sword, judgment, or pestilence, or famine, we will stand before this house and before you—for your name is in this house—and cry out to you in our affliction, and you will hear and save.'

And now behold, the men of Ammon and Moab and Mount Seir, whom you would not let Israel invade when they came from the land of Egypt, and whom they avoided and did not destroy—

behold, they reward us by coming to drive us out of your possession, which you have given us to inherit.

O our God, will you not execute judgment on them? For we are powerless against this great horde that is coming against us. We do not know what to do, but our eyes are on you."

Meanwhile all Judah stood before the Lord, with their little ones, their wives, and their children.

And the Spirit of the Lord came upon Jahaziel the son of Zechariah, son of Benaiah, son of Jeiel, son of Mattaniah, a Levite of the sons of Asaph, in the midst of the assembly.

And he said, "Listen, all Judah and inhabitants of Jerusalem and King Jehoshaphat: Thus says the Lord to you, 'Do not be afraid and do not be dismayed at this great horde, for the battle is not yours but God's.

Tomorrow go down against them. Behold, they will come up by the ascent of Ziz. You will find them at the end of the valley, east of the wilderness of Jeruel.

You will not need to fight in this battle. Stand firm, hold your position, and see the salvation of the Lord on your behalf, O Judah and Jerusalem.' Do not be afraid and do not be dismayed. Tomorrow go out against them, and the Lord will be with you."

Then Jehoshaphat bowed his head with his face to the ground, and all Judah and the inhabitants of Jerusalem fell down before the Lord, worshiping the Lord.

And the Levites, of the Kohathites and the Korahites, stood up to praise the Lord, the God of Israel, with a very loud voice.

And they rose early in the morning and went out into the wilderness of Tekoa. And when they went out, Jehoshaphat stood and said, "Hear me, Judah and inhabitants of Jerusalem! Believe in the Lord your God, and you will be established; believe his prophets, and you will succeed."

And when he had taken counsel with the people, he appointed those who were to sing to the Lord and praise him in holy attire, as they went before the army, and say,

"Give thanks to the Lord,
for his steadfast love endures forever."

And when they began to sing and praise, the Lord set an ambush against the men of Ammon, Moab, and Mount Seir, who had come against Judah, so that they were routed.

For the men of Ammon and Moab rose against the inhabitants of Mount Seir, devoting them to destruction, and when they had made an end of the inhabitants of Seir, they all helped to destroy one another.

When Judah came to the watchtower of the wilderness, they looked toward the horde, and behold, there were dead bodies lying on the ground; none had escaped.

When Jehoshaphat and his people came to take their spoil, they found among them in great numbers goods, clothing, and precious things, which they took for themselves until they could carry no more. They were three days in taking the spoil, it was so much.

On the fourth day they assembled in the Valley of Beracah, for there they blessed the Lord. Therefore the name of that place has been called the Valley of Beracah to this day.

Then they returned, every man of Judah and Jerusalem, and Jehoshaphat at their head, returning to Jerusalem with joy, for the Lord had made them rejoice over their enemies.

They came to Jerusalem with harps and lyres and trumpets, to the house of the Lord.

And the fear of God came on all the kingdoms of the countries when they heard that the Lord had fought against the enemies of Israel.

So the realm of Jehoshaphat was quiet, for his God gave him rest all around.

Scripture taken from the ESV® Bible (The Holy Bible, English Standard Version®), copyright ©2001 by Crossway. Used by permission. All rights reserved.

Prologue

The Sound Before the Storm

I should have been afraid.

Standing on the edge of the battlefield, the morning mist curling around our feet, the hills trembling under the weight of approaching armies — any sane man would have been.

But somehow, there was only the song.

My fingers gripped the polished wood of my lyre, slick with sweat. My heart pounded loud enough to drown out the murmurs of the soldiers behind me. I could not see the enemy yet, but I could hear them — the faint clash of armor, the rumble of boots against dry earth.

And yet, here I stood.
A musician.
A Levite.
A singer, not a soldier.

My father had once told me, "Amariah, your name is no accident. God speaks — and when He speaks, He fulfills. Never doubt the One who called you."

I had believed him then — sitting safely within the temple walls, far from the cry of war.

Belief was easier when the battle was a distant rumor.

It was something else entirely to stand before it, weaponless but for a song.

I drew a breath, steadying trembling hands. The appointed leaders nodded. It was time.

And so we sang.

"Give thanks to the Lord, for His steadfast love endures forever."

Our voices rose into the mist — small at first, fragile as a thread. But the song grew stronger with every breath, every heartbeat.

As we sang, something unseen shifted in the air.

Somewhere beyond the hills, the armies of Moab, Ammon, and Mount Seir began to break apart — not because of swords, but because of a song.

This is the story of how God won the battle — and how He taught a simple musician that the greatest victories are born before the first blow falls.

This is the story of The Warrior's Song.

Part 1

The Call to Worship

"Give thanks to the Lord, for He is good;
His steadfast love endures forever."
— 2 Chronicles 20:21

Chapter One

A Musician, Not a Warrior

Morning at the Temple

The first notes of morning rose with the incense.

Amariah sat cross-legged on the worn stone floor of the outer court, cradling his lyre across his lap. His fingers moved deftly along the strings, tuning each one with a practiced ear as sunlight spilled across the temple's golden columns. A soft hum vibrated in the air — the sacred stillness that always settled before the first song was sung.

He closed his eyes for a moment, breathing in the mingled scents of myrrh, cedarwood, and the faint iron tang of the city waking beyond the temple gates. This was his favorite time — before the bustle of priests and worshipers, before the echoes of sacrifice and commerce. Here, at the edge of dawn, it felt as though heaven itself leaned close to listen.

"You're early again," a familiar voice teased.

Amariah looked up to see Eliashib, an older Levite musician, grinning beneath his short-cropped beard. He carried a hammered dulcimer tucked under one arm and a mischievous glint in his eye.

Amariah smiled. "The strings stretch in the cool air. Better to tune them now than embarrass myself before the others."

Eliashib chuckled, settling onto a low bench nearby. "A wise musician thinks of his offering before the first note is played."

Amariah resumed tuning, but his mind wandered. Today they would lead the morning thanksgiving — psalms of praise and remembrance. Songs his father had once sung. Songs sung by generations before him.
He thought again of his name — *Amariah*.
God has said.
His father had whispered it over him when he was a child, hands rough with years of harp strings and sacrifice.

God has spoken over you, my son. Never forget it. Even when you cannot see it — He is faithful to what He says.

Amariah plucked a final note, satisfied. The lyre sang clear and true.

Today, he would lift his song like a banner — a small echo of the promises spoken long ago.

The first priests entered the court, robed in white linen, their feet moving soundlessly across the stone. Other musicians followed — flute players, harpists, singers — each bearing their instruments like sacred vessels. Quiet greetings passed among them.

In the distance, the city stirred: the creak of cart wheels, the bark of merchants opening stalls, the lowing of oxen bound for sacrifice. Life, ordinary and untroubled, unfurled beneath the growing sun.

Amariah stood, adjusting the strap of his lyre across his shoulder.

From the far side of the court, a group of soldiers lingered in the shadows — iron breastplates catching slivers of light, swords strapped at their sides. One of them, a grizzled man with a scar running from temple to chin, leaned against a pillar, watching.

Amariah met his gaze briefly. The soldier gave a nod — not mocking, but measured, almost respectful — and turned away.

A small unease stirred in Amariah's chest.

It was rare to see soldiers near the temple so early.

But the moment passed. Eliashib struck the opening chord on his dulcimer, and the musicians gathered, falling into place.

Amariah took a steadying breath, lifting his voice with the others:

"Give thanks to the Lord, for He is good;
His steadfast love endures forever."

The sound rose pure and strong, weaving among the columns, lifting toward heaven like smoke from the altar.

For now, there was only the song.

For now, the world still held its breath.

The Song of Thanksgiving

The sound of worship soared into the brightening sky.

Amariah's voice blended with the choir of Levites, weaving a rich tapestry of praise that filled the temple courts. His fingers danced across the lyre strings, each note rising like an offering toward the unseen heavens.

"Give thanks to the Lord, for He is good;

His steadfast love endures forever."

The refrain echoed against the polished stone, wrapping around the great bronze pillars and flowing outward through the open gates of the temple into the waking city.

For a moment, Amariah let himself be carried by it — the simple, steady power of worship.

This was the heart of Judah's strength, he thought. Not its walls or its swords, but this: the steadfast love of their God.

A boy — no older than ten — wandered into the court, barefoot and wide-eyed, clutching a bundle of figs in his arms. He paused near the edge of the singers, captivated by the music.

Amariah caught his eye and smiled. The boy grinned back, swaying in time with the rhythm.

It was in these quiet, unnoticed moments that Amariah felt most alive.

Yet beneath the beauty of the song, a small thread of unease pulled at the edges of his mind.

The soldiers still lingered near the outer walls, speaking in low voices. From time to time, one would glance toward the city gates, as if expecting news.

Amariah tried to push the sight from his thoughts.

Surely it was nothing. Jerusalem was a stronghold. They had faced threats before — wandering raiders, petty kings jealous of Judah's wealth.

None had ever breached the city's defenses. None had ever dared to challenge the house of the living God.

Still, when he plucked the next chord, his hand trembled slightly against the strings.

"For He delivers His people;
His mercy is everlasting."

The boy with the figs dropped one, gasping as it tumbled across the stone and came to rest at Amariah's feet.

Smiling, Amariah bent to retrieve it and offered it back with a wink.

The boy's laughter — pure, unguarded — rippled through the stillness like a promise of better things.

A promise Amariah clung to more tightly than he realized.

As the final notes of the song faded into silence, a hush fell over the court.

It was then — just at the moment when the morning felt most perfect — that the sound of pounding feet broke the spell.

A messenger tore through the temple gates, his cloak flying behind him like a tattered banner, his face pale with exhaustion and fear.

Even before he spoke, Amariah knew.

The battle he had always thought belonged to other men was now rushing toward him.

The Rumor Arrives

The messenger stumbled to a halt at the center of the court, gasping for breath.

His clothes were torn, dust clung to his skin, and a gash bled freely from his forehead. For a heartbeat, no one moved — priests, musicians, temple guards — all frozen in the stunned silence that follows a crash no one thought would come.

The high priest was the first to speak.

"What news?" he demanded, his voice cutting through the thick morning air like a blade.

The messenger bent double, struggling to find words.

"They are coming," he choked out. "A vast multitude... from beyond the sea, from Edom. Moab... Ammon... Mount Seir... they march together."

A ripple of shock ran through the gathered Levites.

Amariah felt his lyre slip slightly in his grasp.

Three armies? Allied together?
That was no raiding party. That was a force of destruction — a tide meant to sweep Judah from the earth.

The high priest pressed forward. "How close?"

The man lifted wide, terrified eyes.
"Already at Hazazon-tamar. Engedi. Days, maybe less."

Murmurs broke out across the court — frantic, disbelieving.

Hazazon-tamar was no longer some distant dot on a trader's map. It was close. Too close.

Amariah's stomach twisted.
They had sung songs of deliverance all morning, but the battle was no longer a poetic metaphor. It was coming like a storm, fast and merciless.

Across the court, a young flutist dropped his instrument with a clatter. An older singer gripped his robes, whispering prayers under his breath. Even the soldiers near the gate stiffened, hands straying instinctively toward their sword hilts.

The world Amariah knew — the world of songs and sacred rhythms, of steady, predictable worship — was unraveling with every heartbeat.

He tightened his hold on the lyre, the wood suddenly feeling brittle beneath his fingers.

I'm not a soldier, he thought, panic rising. *I don't know how to fight.*

Someone shouted for the priests to assemble. Another called for runners to alert the palace. Orders barked, sandals slapped against stone, the temple once filled with music now alive with fear.

Amariah stood in the chaos, unmoving, the rising din around him sounding strangely muffled, as though he were underwater.

His heart beat a frantic rhythm against his ribs.

He was a Levite — a keeper of worship, not a wielder of weapons. His entire life had been one of singing before the altar, not standing before an enemy's sword.

What use was a song against a sword?

Chapter Two
Fear in the Camp

The Fear Spreads

The temple court, once filled with the music of praise, now buzzed with frantic voices.

Amariah pressed his back against a marble pillar, gripping his lyre tightly to his chest as a torrent of news and fear flowed around him.

"Three armies— marching together!"
"They'll reach the city gates before the new moon!"
"Our walls can't hold them!"
"Where is the king? Why hasn't he sent word?"

The words battered Amariah harder than any sword could have. He watched the faces of his fellow musicians — men who had led countless songs of faith — now pale and trembling. Mothers clutched their children. Merchants whispered of fleeing south to Hebron or hiding in the hills.

Even among the temple guards, the mood had shifted.

Where once they had stood relaxed, hands loose at their belts, now they gripped their spears tight, their eyes darting toward the city gates as if expecting the enemy to burst through at any moment.

Amariah caught a snippet of a conversation between two young soldiers near the gate.

"They say their numbers are like the sands of the sea," one muttered, voice low.

The other spat into the dust. "We don't have enough men to hold them back. Not by half."

Amariah swallowed hard, his mouth dry.

He had no sword. No armor. No training for war.

What can I do? he thought bitterly.
What can a singer do against the march of death?

The sun climbed higher, burning away the mist and laying the full weight of the day upon Jerusalem.

And still, no word from the palace. No battle plan. No assurances.

Only a city holding its breath and waiting for the storm to break.

The King's Call to Prayer

A low horn sounded from the palace walls — not the brash blare of a battle cry, but a deeper, slower note. A summons.

Heads turned. Conversations died mid-sentence. Even the birds seemed to fall silent in the heavy noon air.

Amariah looked up, heart hammering.

Another horn answered from the temple gate, then another from the market square. A ripple of sound passed through Jerusalem like a shudder through a body — ancient, solemn, and urgent.

The heralds' voices followed, strong and unwavering.

"All Judah!

Gather at the temple!
Fast and seek the Lord your God!"

A second crier, his voice cracking with strain, repeated the call further down the street.

Soon, the entire city throbbed with the command: not to fight, but to *pray*.

Amariah felt the shift in the air — subtle but real — as fear gave way to something deeper.

Not quite courage.

Not yet hope.

But something stirring from the ashes of panic: a remembrance.

They were the people of the covenant.
This city bore the Name of the living God.
The temple itself was His dwelling place among them.

Slowly, like rivers drawn to a basin, people began streaming toward the temple.

Farmers still dusted from their fields. Merchants abandoning their stalls. Old women leaning on staffs. Young men grim-faced and silent.

Whole families — the old, the young, even the newborns — gathering with solemn faces beneath the banners of Jerusalem.

And at their head, walking not with sword or chariot, but in simple royal robes, came King Jehoshaphat.

Amariah caught his first clear glimpse of the king — a man burdened but not broken.

Jehoshaphat's face was drawn, his steps deliberate.

But there was no arrogance in his bearing, no swagger of kingship.

Only a man leading his people to the only refuge left: the mercy of God.

The king mounted the broad steps before the great bronze doors of the temple.

Behind him, elders and priests stood in solemn ranks.

The crowd gathered in a hushed wave, thousands pressing into the courts, shoulder to shoulder.

Amariah, clutching his lyre close, found himself swept forward by the crush of bodies.
He ended up near a column, close enough to see the strain in Jehoshaphat's hands as he raised them to heaven.

The king's voice, when it rang out over the people, was clear and strong — not the voice of a desperate man, but the voice of one who remembered.

"O Lord, God of our fathers,
Are You not God in heaven?

You rule over all the kingdoms of the nations.
In Your hand are power and might,
So that none is able to withstand You."

The prayer rolled over them like thunder.

Jehoshaphat did not bargain.
He did not boast.
He simply declared the truth: God had delivered them before
— and He could do it again.

Amariah felt the words strike something deep inside him
— something that had withered under fear but now stirred,
cautious and trembling.

"We do not know what to do," the king confessed,
"But our eyes are on You."

The last words hung in the hot air, a fragile thread binding
the people together.

Amariah lowered his head, tears stinging his eyes.
He was still a singer. Still weaponless, armorless.
But maybe — just maybe — that was not the weakness he had
feared.

Maybe it was the point.

The Assembly at the Temple

The assembly stood in silence, thousands holding their breath under the merciless noon sun.

Even the youngest children, who moments before had tugged impatiently at their mothers' sleeves, seemed caught by the solemn stillness.

Then — like the wind stirring after a long drought — a man stepped forward from the ranks of the Levites.

He was not a priest or a soldier. His robe was simple, and his beard shot through with silver.
Amariah recognized him vaguely — Jahaziel, a descendant of Asaph, one of the chief musicians of old.

Jahaziel lifted his face toward the heavens.
When he spoke, it was not with his own voice, but with a power that filled the court like a rushing river.

"Listen, all Judah and inhabitants of Jerusalem and King Jehoshaphat:
Thus says the Lord to you,

*'Do not be afraid and do not be dismayed at this great horde,
for the battle is not yours but God's.
Tomorrow go down against them.
You will not need to fight in this battle.
Stand firm, hold your position, and see the salvation of the Lord
on your behalf.'"*

The words fell like rain upon parched ground.

Amariah felt a tremor run through him — not of fear, but of
something different, something stronger: awe.

The battle was not theirs.
The swords at their sides would not save them.
Neither would the walls, or the gates, or the numbers.

Only the steadfast love of the Lord.

Around him, heads bowed in worship.
Mothers wept.
Soldiers dropped to their knees, weapons clattering against
stone.

Amariah clutched his lyre so tightly that his knuckles turned
white.

Tomorrow, they would march — not with war cries or battle
horns — but with songs of praise.

The very thought made his heart pound with something that
felt dangerously close to courage.

Chapter Three

The Choice to Sing

The Night of Wrestling

The streets of Jerusalem had fallen into uneasy silence.

Torchlight flickered against the heavy stones of the temple walls, casting long shadows that danced like restless spirits in the corners. Somewhere in the distance, a dog barked once — sharp, anxious — before being swallowed by the night.

Amariah sat alone beneath a stone archway, the worn leather strap of his lyre cutting across his chest. He had not played a single note since the assembly ended. His fingers, so sure that morning, now curled into fists.

The city slept — or tried to — but Amariah knew the truth.

Behind shuttered windows and bolted doors, Judah's people huddled with their fears.

Mothers wept quietly into folded hands.

Fathers stared into the dark, wondering if they would live to see another sunrise.

Children clutched their mother's skirts, sensing the fear no words could hide.

And what was he doing?

Amariah clenched his jaw, shame burning in his chest.

"I'm a singer," he thought bitterly.
"A singer. What good is a song against a sword?"

He tilted his head back against the cold stone, staring up into the stars that wheeled silently overhead. The same stars that had witnessed God's covenant with Abraham, Isaac, and Jacob.

Did they still shine for Judah tonight?

Or had God turned His face away?

Amariah wanted to believe the words the prophet Jahaziel had spoken.

"The battle is not yours but God's."

He wanted to believe that their praise could tear down armies like it had toppled the walls of Jericho.

But what if this time was different?

What if tomorrow, he marched to the front of Judah's army with a lyre in his hands — and was the first to die?

The thought twisted in his gut like a knife.

He dropped his head into his hands.

"God, I don't know how to do this," he prayed silently, desperate. *"I'm not strong. I'm not brave. I don't even know if I can sing when the enemy is staring me down."*

No thunder answered him.
No great vision appeared in the night sky.
Only the faint, steady crackle of torches and the endless, indifferent stars.

Slowly, Amariah lifted his head.

The name whispered through his memory — the name his father had given him, the name spoken over him like a blessing and a prophecy.

Amariah.

"God has said."

Not *might say.*
Not *once said long ago but has since forgotten.*
God has said.
And when God speaks, the world bends to His word.

Amariah reached for his lyre with shaking hands.

The wood felt too light to be a shield, too fragile to be a sword.

But somehow — somehow — it was the only weapon he had been given.

He pulled his fingers across the strings, and a soft, trembling note rose into the night.

It was not much.

It was not strong.

But it was enough.

A quiet melody found its way into the darkness, weaving between the stones, rising toward heaven like a prayer too deep for words.

"Even if I cannot see the victory," Amariah thought, *"I will sing."*

"Even if I do not understand the battle, I will trust the One who fights for me."

Tomorrow, he would march at the head of Judah's army.
Not with armor or sword.
But with a song.

And tonight, that song began here —
In the place where fear bowed to faith.

Night of Surrender

The stars burned cold and silent over Jerusalem.

Amariah sat near the outer courtyard, the smooth stone cool beneath him, the torches guttering low. His lyre rested in his lap, silent but heavy, a familiar weight that had never felt so unfamiliar before.

All around him, the city slept uneasily, the shadows thick with unspoken fear.

He bowed his head, pressing his forehead against the polished wood of his instrument.

"I am not a warrior," he whispered into the night. *"I am only a singer."*

He had thought the battle would be fought with shields and spears, strength against strength.

Instead, he was being asked to walk forward with nothing but a song.

It made no sense.
It defied reason.
It demanded faith deeper than anything he had ever known.

Amariah tightened his grip on the lyre until his knuckles whitened.

"God, help me," he prayed.
"Help me believe when fear claws at my throat. Help me stand when my heart trembles. Help me sing when the enemy is near."

He lifted the lyre slowly.

Not because the fear had vanished.
But because obedience meant trusting in the One who had spoken.

Amariah.
God has said.

He strummed a single chord — soft, trembling — but it rose into the night like a prayer.

No armies moved yet.
No miracles split the sky.

Only a boy with a lyre and a broken hallelujah, lifted to the heavens in faith.

Tomorrow, the king would call them to march.

Tomorrow, he would stand at the front lines with nothing but a song.

But tonight — here, in the stillness — the real battle was already being won.

Amariah would sing.

Whatever came, he would trust the voice that had spoken from the beginning of all things.

And that was enough.

Reflection Before the Fast

The city had fallen into an uneasy hush.

Amariah slipped away from the crowded streets, weaving between narrow stone alleys that led to the eastern wall of Jerusalem. His feet scuffed the dust, but he barely noticed. His heart thundered too loudly for him to hear anything else.

He reached a small, quiet place — a corner of the city wall where a few wild vines clung stubbornly to the cracks — and sank to his knees.

For the first time since the rumors of war had reached the temple gates, he let the fear show on his face.

He pressed his forehead to the rough stone, the chill of it biting against his skin.

"God of our fathers," he whispered, voice cracking, *"what are we to do?"*

The words tumbled out of him — unpracticed, unpolished, raw.

"You who parted the sea for Moses... You who gave David victory over Goliath... Have You left us now?"

He clenched his fists against the ground, gravel biting into his palms.

"I am no soldier," he said, the confession thick in his throat. *"I have no sword, no shield. Only a song. Only my hands and my voice."*

A gust of wind stirred the vines, whispering along the stones.

Amariah closed his eyes.

"If we fast, will You hear? If we pray, will You see? If we lift our voices, will You still answer from heaven?"

He waited, heart pounding.

The heavens gave no thunderous reply.
The earth did not shake.
The city remained cloaked in stillness.

But somewhere deep inside — deeper than fear, deeper than the questions — a memory stirred:

God has said.

He did not always shout above the storms.
He often spoke in stillness, through promises already made.

Amariah pushed himself upright slowly.

His legs trembled, but his heart had found a thread to hold onto — fragile but real.

"We will fast," he whispered. *"We will pray. And if You are still the God we have heard of... we will see Your hand again."*

He lifted his lyre — not to play, but to cradle it close against his heart like a shield of faith — and turned back toward the temple.

Toward the king.
Toward the fast.
Toward whatever awaited them in the courts of the Lord.

Selah

The Call to Worship

Before the first sword was raised, before the battle lines were drawn, there was a call — a call not to arms, but to faith.

Amariah lived in the safety of worship, believing his songs would always rise in peace.

But the day came when fear breached the walls of Jerusalem, and the songs of the temple were weighed against the threats of armies.

As panic spread and doubts took root, the King of Judah did not call for swords.

He called for fasting.
For prayer.
For a return to the God who had always been their defender.

In the stillness of the temple courts, a trembling people heard a breathtaking word:

"The battle is not yours, but God's."

It was not swords that would lead Judah into battle.

It was songs.

And in the quiet of the night, before the dawn of war, a young musician named Amariah made his choice.

He would not lift a blade.

He would lift his voice.

Because God had spoken — and that was enough.

*Turn the page, and march into the battle where
worship leads the way.*

Part 2

Worship as Warfare

"You will not need to fight in this battle. Stand firm, hold your position, and see the salvation of the Lord on your behalf."
— 2 Chronicles 20:17

Chapter Four
Morning March

The March Begins

The road wound downward from Jerusalem like a pale ribbon unfurling in the dawn.

Amariah marched at the front of the procession, the lyre light against his back, the song steady on his lips.

Around him, the other musicians sang in full voice, the words as natural now as breathing:

"Give thanks to the Lord,
for His steadfast love endures forever."

Thousands moved behind them — soldiers, farmers, merchants, craftsmen — an army not clad in glittering steel, but in homespun tunics and leather sandals, their faces turned upward, their voices lifted in faith.

The morning air was crisp, carrying the scent of olive groves and dry dust. The rhythm of their footsteps drummed a steady pulse into the earth — a heartbeat of faith pressing against the coming storm.

Amariah stole a glance at the hills rising ahead, mist curling low along their slopes.

Beyond those hills, somewhere just out of sight, the enemy waited.

He tightened his grip on his lyre, heart pounding.

"Steadfast love," he whispered under his breath.
"Steadfast love, not our strength."

The priests who led the march carried no swords.
Only trumpets of silver and hearts set on the God of their fathers.

King Jehoshaphat walked a few paces behind the musicians, head bowed in prayer, his voice rising at times above the song to proclaim the promises of the Lord.

As the sun climbed higher, Amariah began to see the first signs of devastation.

Trampled fields.

Abandoned carts, broken and scattered along the road.

A farmhouse, its doors hanging from broken hinges, eerily silent.

Fear prickled at the edge of his mind.

"Was this what awaited us too?" he thought.

He squeezed his eyes shut for a moment, anchoring himself to the rhythm of the song.

"Give thanks to the Lord..."
"Give thanks to the Lord..."

He opened them again to find Eliashib, the elder musician, glancing at him with a tight, knowing smile. Without a word, the older man struck a chord on his dulcimer, louder, more certain.

Amariah smiled back.

The song strengthened.

Closer to the Enemy

The road crested a low hill, and the valley beyond unfurled like a battlefield waiting to be claimed.

And there — sprawled across the plains like a sea of iron and leather — were the enemy armies.

Even from this distance, the sight made Amariah's breath catch in his throat.

Thousands upon thousands.
Banners fluttering.
Weapons gleaming in the sunlight.
The ground itself seemed to tremble under their sheer numbers.

A collective gasp passed through Judah's ranks.

For a heartbeat, the song faltered.

A tremor of fear moved through the musicians, through the soldiers, through Amariah himself.

"Steadfast love endures forever..."
"Steadfast love..."

The words stumbled in his mouth.

It would be so easy to turn back.
So easy to let fear choke the song before it reached the enemy's ears.

But then —
King Jehoshaphat's voice rang out behind them, firm and unshaken:

"Stand firm, hold your position, and see the salvation of the Lord!"

A trumpet sounded — clear and bright.

Amariah drew a breath, filling his lungs with air sharper than any blade, and lifted his voice again.

Stronger this time.

"Give thanks to the Lord,
for His steadfast love endures forever."

The song swelled.
One voice. Then another. Then the army behind them, picking up the refrain with a ferocity born not of numbers, but of faith.

The enemy camp had noticed them now — a ripple of motion passing through their ranks like the first stirrings of a storm.

Amariah's heart beat wildly in his chest.

Still, he sang.

The musicians stepped forward, not with weapons drawn, but with songs rising to heaven —
their worship louder than their fear.

Step by step, note by note, they advanced into the valley.

Into the arms of a miracle yet unseen.

Chapter Five
Songs in the Mist

The Enemy Turns

The mist hung low over the valley, veiling the enemy camp in a ghostly shroud.

Amariah stood with the other musicians at the crest of the hill, their song pouring out into the heavy morning air.

"Give thanks to the Lord,
for His steadfast love endures forever."

The refrain rose and fell like the beating of wings.

Below them, the vast armies of Moab, Ammon, and Mount Seir shifted restlessly, banners stirring in the thin breeze.

Amariah could see the glitter of armor, the sharp glint of spear tips.

But something was wrong.

The enemy camp seethed — not with the ordered discipline of an army preparing for battle, but with growing confusion.

Cries echoed across the valley — sharp, angry, disjointed.

Figures moved chaotically, shoving and gesturing wildly.
Lines broke apart.
Shields clashed not against an advancing foe, but against each other.

Amariah's voice faltered for a heartbeat, stunned.

What was happening?

Beside him, Eliashib gasped, eyes wide.

"They're fighting each other," he whispered.

Amariah strained to see through the mist.

It was true.

The armies of Moab and Ammon — who had come together to destroy Judah — were now turning their swords against the men of Mount Seir.
The alliance crumbled into bloodshed.

Screams rose into the morning air, and the ground itself seemed to tremble — not with the march of an army, but with the chaos of betrayal.

Amariah gripped his lyre tighter.

"Keep singing," he told himself. *"Keep singing."*

The musicians pressed forward with the song, voices quivering but unbroken.

"Give thanks to the Lord,
for His steadfast love endures forever."

The enemy camp dissolved into madness.

Swords flashed in the mist.
Banners toppled.
Shouts turned to shrieks.

The armies that had once looked like an unstoppable flood were tearing themselves apart — not by Judah's strength, but by the invisible hand of the Lord.

Amariah felt a shiver run down his spine.

This was no accident.
No trick of military strategy.

This was the power of the living God answering the faith of His people.

Awe and Amazement

The song faltered again, not from fear this time, but from awe.

Amariah and the musicians stood frozen at the top of the ridge, watching as the valley below became a graveyard.

Not a single man from Judah had lifted a sword.
Not one.

It was the enemy's own rage — their own confusion — that had destroyed them.

The sun broke fully over the horizon, burning away the mist in golden shafts of light.

The devastation became clear.

Bodies lay strewn across the fields.
Shields and spears littered the ground like fallen leaves.
Where once had stood three mighty armies, there was now only silence.

The priests began to weep openly.
The soldiers behind them dropped to their knees, faces to the ground.

Amariah lowered his lyre slowly, reverently.

He had expected to die this day.

Instead, he had witnessed a miracle.

He closed his eyes, lifting his face toward the morning sky.

"Steadfast love," he whispered.
"Steadfast love endures forever."

The song rose again — this time not as a weapon of warfare, but as a song of overwhelming praise.

It flowed down the hillside, across the broken valley, up into the heavens — a declaration that no enemy could silence:

"Give thanks to the Lord,
for His steadfast love endures forever."

And in the light of the new day, Judah stood victorious — not by the might of their hands, but by the power of their praise.

Chapter Six

The Battle Breaks

A Valley of Silence

Amariah stood at the crest of the hill, lyre dangling from his hand, as the last curls of mist lifted from the valley below.

The battlefield was eerily silent.

No trumpets of victory.
No clash of final blows.
Only the soft rustle of the breeze over a valley littered with the fallen.

Amariah swallowed hard.

The armies that had once promised to destroy Judah lay broken — not by Judah's strength, but by the invisible hand of the Almighty.

He stepped forward carefully, reverently, as though walking on sacred ground.

Others followed — priests, soldiers, elders — moving slowly among the wreckage.
There was no need for swords.
There was no enemy left to fight.

Here and there, the mist caught glints of silver and gold scattered among the ruins — abandoned shields inlaid with precious metals, chests of supplies, ornate weapons dropped in haste and confusion.

Treasures meant for destruction now lay at Judah's feet.

Amariah knelt beside a shattered shield, tracing the edge of it with his fingers.

"This is not our victory," he thought. *"This is God's mercy."*

The Days of Gathering Spoils

The valley stretched wide beneath the afternoon sun, no longer veiled in mist, no longer filled with armies, but with the remnants of what had once been a flood of destruction.

Amariah knelt beside an overturned chariot, brushing away the dust to reveal a chest studded with hammered silver.

He had never seen such wealth with his own eyes before.
And yet, as he traced the filigree patterns along the chest's edge, he felt no greed stir in his heart — only reverence.

This was not a reward they had earned.

This was a testimony they had been entrusted to carry.

Around him, the people moved quietly among the ruins — gathering fine robes, coins, weapons, shields inlaid with jewels.
There were no shouts of triumph.
No boasting.

Only awe.

The musicians moved among them, lyres strapped to their backs, flutes tucked into belts, dulcimers slung over shoulders.

Songs still rose in low voices — not performance now, but gratitude.

"Give thanks to the Lord,
for His steadfast love endures forever."

It took an entire day to gather what could be easily carried.

When the carts were filled and the sun began to fall, they made camp at the valley's edge, cooking small meals over low fires and singing as the stars bloomed overhead.

The next day, they returned — and the next.

For three full days, they labored, carrying treasures from a battlefield where no man of Judah had needed to raise a sword.

On the second morning, Amariah paused near the remnants of a fallen standard — the broken banner of a once-proud army. At its base lay a sword.

It was a beautiful thing — a masterwork of iron and bronze, its hilt wrapped in leather so fine it seemed to glow in the light.

He picked it up carefully.

The blade was sharp, but its purpose was finished.

Amariah turned it over in his hands, then laid it across the broken banner, a silent offering to the lesson the valley had taught him:

Strength without God was weakness.
Victory without worship was impossible.

He lifted his lyre once more and walked on.

The valley was no longer a place of fear.

It had become a field of remembrance.

And Judah — every son, every daughter — would remember who had fought for them.

The Triumphant Return

When the day came to return to Jerusalem, the people gathered in ranks once more.

Not as soldiers.

But as worshipers.

Amariah stood at the head of the musicians again, lyre in hand, voice steady.

King Jehoshaphat led the procession — not crowned in bloodshed, but robed in thanksgiving.

The trumpeters sounded the call.
The singers lifted the song.
The priests marched forward with banners raised high, bearing the names of the tribes of Judah.

The valley behind them — once a place of death — now whispered only of God's faithfulness.

Amariah sang until his voice cracked.

He sang for the fear he had once felt.
He sang for the miracle he had witnessed.
He sang for the steadfast love that had proven stronger than the armies of men.

As they approached the gates of Jerusalem, the city answered them — crowds pouring out to meet them with shouts of joy, tambourines clashing, children waving branches in the air.

The whole city shook not with fear, but with celebration.

The temple gates swung open wide, and the people streamed in, lifting praise higher than the tallest towers.

Amariah caught sight of the little boy who had once dropped a fig at his feet — now perched on his father's shoulders, clapping his hands wildly in rhythm with the song.

Tears blurred Amariah's vision.

He lifted his face toward heaven, letting the last notes of the song pour out of him like a river returning to the sea.

"Give thanks to the Lord," he cried, voice ragged and full, *"for His steadfast love endures forever!"*

And the people answered him with a roar that shook the heavens.

Selah

Worship as Warfare

The armies of Judah did not march with sharpened swords or iron shields.

They marched with songs — songs that rose like banners against the unseen.

When fear had every right to rule their hearts, they chose worship.
When the enemy gathered in overwhelming force, they chose faith.
And when they could have trusted in their own strength, they lifted their eyes — and their voices — to the One who had never failed them.

The valley that should have become their grave became the stage for a miracle.

The battlefield that should have swallowed their future became the place where God's power thundered unseen through the mist.

Because worship was never a performance.
It was never meant to stay within temple walls.

Worship was their warfare.
Their trust was their triumph.
Their song was their sword.

And without lifting a blade, Judah stood victorious —
because they chose to believe that the God who had spoken would be faithful to His Word.

The battle was over — but the legacy of worship was just beginning.

Part 3

The Legacy of Worship

"One generation shall commend your works to another, and shall declare your mighty acts."
— Psalm 145:4

Chapter Seven

Songs for Tomorrow

A New Song Rising

The smoke from the altar drifted into the evening sky, twisting like ribbons of praise.

Amariah stood near the temple courtyard once more, the familiar weight of his lyre resting against his side.

But tonight, the air buzzed with a different kind of energy — not fear, not tension — but joy.

Everywhere he looked, there was life.

Children chased each other between the pillars, their laughter ringing where once there had been whispered prayers of desperation.

Merchants filled the streets again, their carts overflowing with grain and oil, with fabrics dyed in colors that gleamed in the sun.

Old men leaned on their staffs, telling and retelling the story of the valley — the valley where they had seen a miracle with their own eyes.

And in every doorway, in every market square, the same song could be heard:

"Give thanks to the Lord,
for His steadfast love endures forever."

The song had become more than a battle cry.
It had become the anthem of a generation.

Amariah plucked a soft chord on his lyre, letting the notes float upward.
He smiled as a group of younger Levites gathered near, instruments in hand, waiting for him to lead.

He saw himself in their eager eyes — saw the same nervous hope, the same hungry faith.

But something had changed.

They were not singing out of tradition alone.

They were singing from a place of remembrance — a place carved deep by the hand of God.

Amariah straightened, his heart swelling.

Worship had not ended with the victory.

Worship had become their way of life.

He drew a deep breath and raised his voice once more, not as a boy clinging to obedience, but as a man leading a new generation to remember.

"Give thanks to the Lord," he sang,
"for His steadfast love endures forever."

The courtyard answered him, rising like a tide of living praise.

And far beyond the city walls, in every field, in every village, the song echoed — a testimony written not on scrolls alone, but on hearts forever changed by the power of worship.

Teaching the New Song

The courtyard was quieter now.

The festival of praise had ended days ago, but the heart of worship still pulsed through the stones. Morning light poured over the eastern wall of the temple, painting the marble in hues of gold.

Amariah sat cross-legged near the outer colonnade, surrounded once more by young Levites — the same ones who had gathered with him in firelight weeks ago.

But today, they weren't just learning.

They were creating.

Scrolls lay unfurled around them, some marked with faded psalms, others with blank parchment and fresh ink. One of the boys tapped out a soft rhythm on a hand drum, while a girl hummed a melody, half-formed but full of something ancient and new.

They were writing a new song — a song that would tell the story of the valley.

Amariah listened as the youngest girl recited her line nervously:

*"He threw confusion on the enemy's face, and led
us out by mercy, not by might."*

The others nodded, murmuring approval.

Amariah smiled gently.

"Truth before rhyme," he said. "Let the words carry what we
saw, not just what sounds good."

Another boy scribbled a new line quickly:

*"We did not fight. We did not run. We only stood
— and worship won."*

They all turned to Amariah.

He looked down at the lyre resting beside him — the same
one he had carried into the valley.
The same one he thought might be the last thing he ever held.

He strummed a quiet chord.

Then another.

And then, gently, he sang:

*"Your love, O Lord, a banner raised, Your faith-
fulness our shield. We sang, and You destroyed the
threat — Your mercy won the field."*

The courtyard stilled. Even the breeze paused.

The children stared at him, wide-eyed.

Amariah set his lyre down slowly.

"That's what we remember," he said softly. "Not that we
survived — but that He fought. And He was enough."

The youngest among them nodded slowly, her fingers curling
around her own small lyre.

They spent the rest of the morning threading lyrics together,
building verse by verse — a memorial in melody, a testimony in
harmony.

And when the sun reached its peak, the new song was finished.

It would be sung at the temple.
It would be taught in homes.
It would echo through hills and villages for years to come.

A song for the next generation.

A song of the God who fights for His people — when they choose to sing.

Chapter Eight

The Song Continues

A Festival of Praise

The streets of Jerusalem were alive with music.

Banners rippled in the breeze, woven with threads of gold and scarlet, catching the morning light. The gates of the temple stood wide open, welcoming throngs of worshipers pouring in from every corner of Judah — farmers and merchants, soldiers and singers, children and elders alike.

Today was not a day of mourning.
Today was a day of remembering.

Amariah stood on the wide steps of the temple courtyard, lyre in hand, gazing out over the sea of faces. His heart felt too full for words.

It had been months since the valley had fallen silent, months since the Lord had fought the battle on their behalf. Yet the memory burned as brightly as if it were yesterday.

They had not forgotten.

They had come to celebrate the faithfulness of the Lord, not with feasting alone, but with *songs that still rose like banners against the unseen.*

The Levites were assembled in ranks, their instruments gleaming in the sun. Trumpeters stood ready at the sides of the courtyard, their silver horns aimed heavenward. Choirs of singers, young and old, filled the steps leading to the inner court, each heart beating with the same purpose:

To declare that God had won the battle —
and that His steadfast love endures forever.

King Jehoshaphat, robed in white linen, stood at the forefront, hands lifted in praise, face radiant with thanksgiving.

Amariah adjusted the strap of his lyre, feeling the smooth wood warm against his palm.

He had once questioned whether a song could stand against an army.

Now he knew.

Worship had not only defended a city — it had redefined it.
It had reshaped a people.
It had rebuilt hope.

At a signal from the high priest, the trumpeters lifted their horns.

The first notes rang out — clear, bold, fearless.

Amariah struck the opening chord of the psalm, and the singers followed:

"Give thanks to the Lord,
for His steadfast love endures forever."

The sound thundered through the courtyard, echoing off the stones, rising into the sky.
It was not a performance.
It was a declaration.

A covenant renewed.

A promise remembered.

A legacy carried forward on the wings of song.

Legacy Secured

Later, as the sun dipped low and the last chords of praise floated into the deepening twilight, Amariah sat quietly beneath one of the great cedars by the temple gate.

Children played nearby, chasing each other with laughter that danced like music in the warm evening air.

In his lap, his lyre rested — worn now from countless songs, but still strong, still true.

A young boy approached shyly, a small flute clutched in his hands.

"Master Amariah?" he asked, his voice hesitant. "Will you teach me to play?"

Amariah smiled, motioning for the boy to sit.

He placed a gentle hand on the child's shoulder and nodded.

"Yes," he said softly. "I will teach you to play."

He looked beyond the boy — past the temple walls, past the city gates — into the endless horizon where battles would come and go, kingdoms would rise and fall, but one truth would remain:

The steadfast love of the Lord endures forever.

And there would always be songs rising to tell the story.

Amariah strummed a soft, steady chord, and together, they began.

The song continued.

Selah

The Legacy of Worship

The battle was won — but the true victory echoed far beyond a single day.

It echoed in the songs that rose in every street, in the laughter of children who knew the story by heart, in the hands of young musicians who tuned their instruments not for performance, but for praise.

Worship had not been a moment.
It had become a movement.

The legacy left by those who chose to sing when fear demanded silence became the foundation for a generation — and for every generation after.

Because when the people of God lift their voices in faith,
when they choose to worship through trembling hands and tear-stained faces,

when they declare God's steadfast love in the valleys as well as
the victories —

they build altars that time cannot erode.

They light fires that darkness cannot extinguish.

They sing songs that battles cannot silence.

The song that rose in the valley would rise forever.

Because the God who fought for them would never fail.

And the worship of His people would never cease.

The battle ended.
The worship never will.

Epilogue
The Song Remains

Years had worn grooves into the stone streets of Jerusalem, but the song still rose like the morning sun.

Amariah sat beneath the shade of an olive tree near the temple courtyard, the old lyre resting across his lap. His hands, once nimble and strong, bore the tremble of time now. His beard, once dark, had silvered like the mist that used to curl over the battlefield he still dreamed of sometimes.

He closed his eyes and listened.

The laughter of children echoed from the temple steps — familiar and wild and full of life.

Beyond the gates, merchants called to one another, and somewhere nearby, a flute trilled a melody that had not been invented when Amariah was young.

And rising above it all — a song he knew by heart.

"Give thanks to the Lord,
for His steadfast love endures forever."

Amariah opened his eyes and smiled.

The same refrain.
The same truth.

The young Levites had gathered near the altar, tuning their instruments, arranging their voices in practice for another festival day.

The faces were new, the robes brighter, the songs laced with new melodies — but the heartbeat remained the same.

The steadfast love of the Lord.

A small boy — no older than five — scampered across the courtyard with a hand-carved lyre clutched in both arms.

The instrument was too large for him.

The notes he plucked were clumsy and wild.

But he sang at the top of his lungs, not caring who heard:

"We did not fight. We did not run.
We only stood — and worship won."

Amariah chuckled, a sound rich with wonder.

He let his fingers drift across the strings of his own lyre, the notes old and familiar, rising to meet the boy's untamed melody.

The boy heard him and grinned, racing over.

"Will you teach me?" he asked, breathless.

Amariah looked into the boy's shining eyes — eyes so full of the future — and nodded.

"Yes," he said, voice soft but steady. "I will teach you."

Because the song was not his alone.

It never had been.

It belonged to every voice willing to believe, to every heart willing to lift worship higher than fear.

It belonged to the generations yet to come —
to the fields yet to face their own battles —
to the valleys yet to be crossed.

Amariah struck a chord — low, sure, and sweet — and the boy joined him, their notes rising together into the sky where the memory of miracles lived.

The song remained.

And it would never be silenced.

Devotional Companion

Worship Through the Battle

These five reflections are inspired by the journey of Amariah and the people of Judah in The Warrior's Song. May they strengthen your own worship as you walk through valleys, battles, and victories.

Devotional 1:

Sing Before You See

"We walk by faith, not by sight." — 2 Corinthians
5:7

Reflection:

Amariah and the musicians of Judah began their march not when the victory was visible, but when the outcome was still hidden in mist. Their worship rose *before* the enemy fell, before deliverance was obvious.

Faith calls us to sing when the outcome is uncertain.
To trust when our eyes see only danger.
To lift worship when fear whispers to stay silent.

Because victory begins when God's people believe His Word — not when the walls fall down.

Reflection Question:

Where is God calling you to worship before you see His hand move?

Devotional 2:

Worship in the Valley

"Even though I walk through the valley of the shadow of death, I will fear no evil, for You are with me." — Psalm 23:4

Reflection:

The valley where Judah faced the enemy could have become their grave. Instead, it became the place where God's power was revealed.

We often pray to be led around valleys.
But what if God's greatest miracles are waiting *inside* them?

Worship transforms valleys into places of victory — because worship keeps our eyes fixed on the One who never fails.

Prayer Thought:

Lord, help me lift my song even in the valleys where fear and shadows dwell. Remind me that You are always with me.

Devotional 3:

Stand Firm and Sing

"You will not need to fight in this battle. Stand firm, hold your position, and see the salvation of the Lord." — 2 Chronicles 20:17

Reflection:

God's command to Judah was not to charge, not to retreat — but to stand and sing.

In the battles of life, standing firm feels harder than running or fighting.
It demands faith rooted deeper than circumstances.
It demands a song louder than fear.
Sometimes standing firm *is* your warfare.
Sometimes singing in surrender *is* your greatest victory.

Reflection Question:

In what area of your life is God calling you to stand firm and keep singing?

Devotional 4:

Victory Belongs to the Lord

"The horse is made ready for the day of battle, but the victory belongs to the Lord." — Proverbs 21:31

Reflection:

Amariah and the people prepared their hearts, not their swords.

Their victory came not from strategy, strength, or skill — but from obedience and worship.

Victory, true victory, is never earned.
It is received by those who trust in the faithfulness of their God.

The pressure is not on you to win.
The calling is on you to believe, worship, and walk faithfully.

Prayer Thought:

Father, help me release the battles I cannot win on my own, and trust that You are fighting for me.

Devotional 5:

Songs for the Next Generation

"One generation shall commend Your works to another, and shall declare Your mighty acts." —
Psalm 145:4

Reflection:

Amariah's greatest legacy was not the battle he survived — it was the song he taught.

When we choose to worship through fear, through uncertainty, through trials, we pass on a story that outlives us.

A song that others will need when their own valleys loom ahead.

The songs we sing today are seeds planted in the soil of tomorrow.

Reflection Question:

What song of faith are you leaving for the next generation to sing?

Acknowledgements

Worship has been the thread woven through my life since childhood. I come from a rich heritage of music and ministry — a family that didn't just sing, but lived lives of worship.

I began playing piano in church when I was just eight years old, shaped by the sounds and songs of faith that filled our home. My Mema, Marion Williams, was one of the first people who truly taught me what it meant to worship. She didn't just play hymns — she lived them, and her example planted something in me that still grows today.

My parents — Sheila and the late Gene Howard — made worship a part of our daily life. Even in grief, worship was our language. When my dad passed away in 1993, I was only eleven. I can still remember sitting around the piano in our living room with my extended family, singing through the pain, the heartache, and the valley of loss. Even then, I knew the power of worship. I knew that the song could carry us where words could not.

To my mom and stepdad, the late Dennis Minix — thank you for loving me, supporting me, and believing in the call God placed on my life. Dennis never played an instrument, but his heart for worship and the way he loved me still carries me through every day. Your encouragement gave me the courage to follow God's leading, even when the path was hard to understand.

I am forever grateful to Pastor Chucky Chandler, who recently went home to be with the Lord. He believed in a young kid with a call on his life, and I carry his voice with me every time I step into a moment of worship. To Bishop Richard Martin and Bishop Eddie Crocker, thank you for your encouragement, prayers, and steady presence through the years. You saw God's hand on me before I could see it myself.

"Since we are surrounded by so great a cloud of witnesses..."
I can run into battle with worship as my weapon because these men and women of God showed me how.

To my team — the choir and band of First Baptist Church of the Islands — thank you for being more than musicians. You are warriors. I've seen you lead not just with talent but with heart, conviction, and courage. You've reminded me again and again that worship truly is warfare — and I'm honored to stand with you.

And most of all — to my Heavenly Father. You took what little I had, and You used it. You continue to shape me, teach me, and call me deeper. It is the joy of my life to be a worshiper and a warrior for Your Kingdom.

I don't have a sword.
I don't wear armor.
But I have a song.

And that's more than enough.

About the Author

 Adam Howard serves as the Worship Pastor at First Baptist Church of the Islands in Savannah, Georgia, where he daily witnesses the beauty of grace, second chances, and stories rewritten by the Savior.

He is the author of *Heart of Faith*, a powerful journey through endurance, healing, and unwavering trust in God; *Barabbas: Redeemed by Innocence*, a raw and redemptive exploration of mercy and new life; and *The Warrior's Song*, a moving call to worship as the weapon of the faithful.

Adam is also the creator of *The Bristo Hudson Chronicles*, an imaginative, spiritually rich fiction series for young readers. Through adventure, mystery, and deep character journeys, the series invites readers to explore timeless truths about identity, courage, legacy, and God's presence in both the extraordinary and the everyday.

Across all his writing, Adam weaves a single thread:
Stories that reflect the heart of the Gospel — real, raw, and redeeming.

He lives in Savannah, Georgia, with his wife, Marcia, and their two children, Ben and Lilli. When he's not writing, leading worship, or building new stories, he loves spending time with his family, exploring coastal trails, and chasing the wonder in everyday moments.

Stay tuned — new titles are already in the works!

To learn more, explore new releases, and join Adam's reader community, visit: **www.adamhowardministries.com**

Sign up for Adam's newsletter to receive updates, behind-the-scenes looks at upcoming books, and encouragement for your own journey of faith and worship.

Stay Connected

The journey doesn't end here. If this book spoke to you, encouraged your faith, or stirred your heart, I would love to hear from you.

You can reach out to me directly at **adam@adamhowar dministries.com** — because your story matters. Your voice matters.

Let's keep walking the road of redemption — together.

If you'd like to stay connected for future books, devotionals, and behind-the-scenes encouragement, you can sign up for my newsletter at **www.adamhowardministries.com**.

You'll receive updates on upcoming releases, including new titles in *The Bristo Hudson Chronicles*, faith-filled resources, devotionals, events, and more words to strengthen your journey.